To our boys, Isaac and Ezra

Heart of a Snowman
Text copyright © 2009 by Mary Kuryla and Eugene Yelchin
Illustrations copyright © 2009 by Eugene Yelchin

Manufactured in China.
Library of Congress Cataloging-in-Publication Data is available.
ISBN 978-0-06-125926-5 (trade bdg.)

Typography by Martha Rago
09 10 11 12 13 LEO 10 9 8 7 6 5 4 3 2 1 ❖ First Edition

Heart
of a
SnowMan

by **Mary Kuryla** *and* **Eugene Yelchin**

HarperCollins*Publishers*

Owen knew that at the heart of a snowman is a perfect snowball. To make a perfect snowball, you need the powdery kind of snow that's a touch melty. Owen packed handfuls of it into a round ball and rolled the ball around, this way and that. And so he rolled it into something large.

"You make the best snowmen," said Owen's little sister. "His eyes are looking at me."

Owen smiled with pride. "Those aren't eyes. They're buttons."

His sister dug a carrot from her pocket and handed it to him. It was twisted and thin. He took it anyway.

"How will you keep him warm?"

"He doesn't need to be warm," said Owen. "He's cold all the way through."

"But he's warm inside," she said, sure of it.

Owen was too busy to argue. He looked at her scarf. "He could use that."

His sister's hand went up to her scarf. The knitting gaped in great holes the way only comfy scarves do. "Okay, you can have it," she said. "I won't need it tomorrow. There's going to be lots of sun."

Every year Owen built a snowman on Christmas Eve,
but the sun always melted it by Christmas Day. There's
got to be a way to keep it around, Owen told himself.

chimney. Owen was so worried about his snowman
he didn't even notice.

Long after bedtime, a brilliant light beamed down on Owen's snowman. It came from a vessel hovering overhead. Owen ran out of the house and called, "What are you doing with my snowman?" He grabbed hold of his snowman and was pulled inside.

Within the vessel, it was still and hushed as fallen snow.
Snowmen pressed in on every side. In the distance, Owen
saw steam pumping up from a factory all shiny and bright.

Owen and his snowman were abruptly ejected from the
vessel into a vast factory.

"Please step away from your snowman," said a chilling voice
on a loudspeaker. "You're too warm, Owen."

Piece by piece, Owen's snowman was carried off along
smooth tubes. Owen felt hot with anger in spite of the terrible
cold in the factory. They were unmaking his snowman!

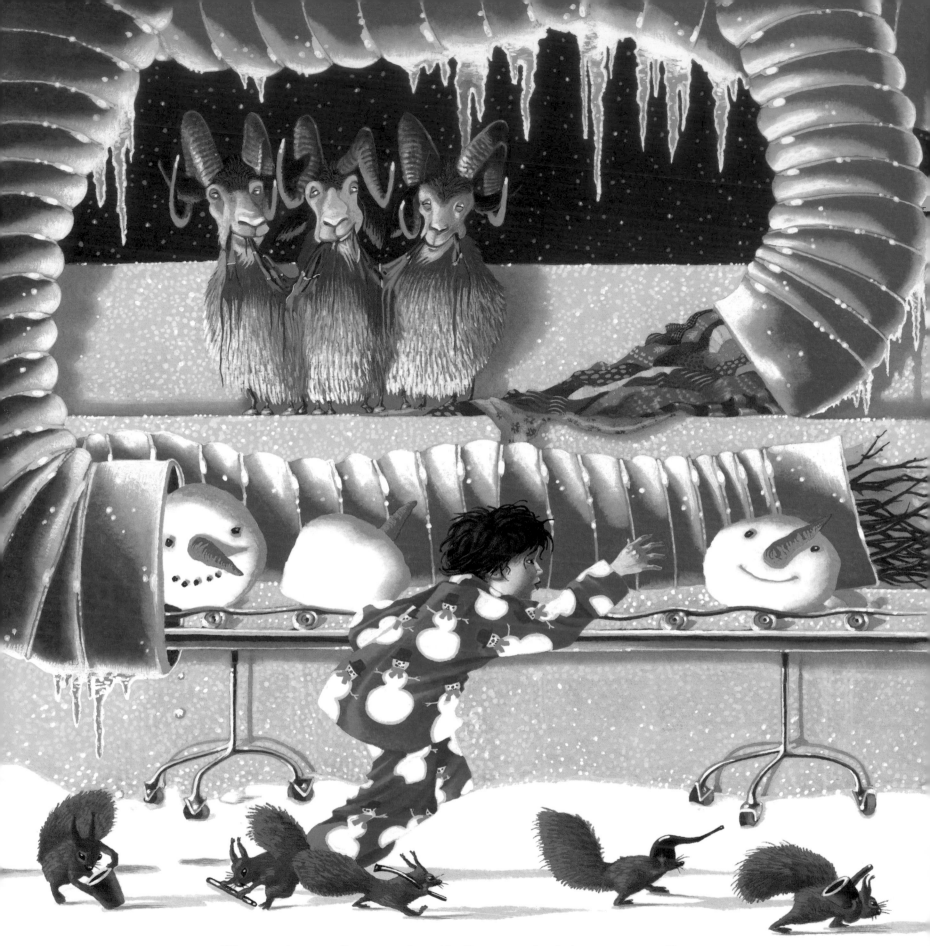

The next room hummed with the sound of destruction. Owen saw his snowman's head placed on a conveyor belt. The rabbit's job was to eat the nose. He was good at his job.

Steadily, steadily went the woolies, unknitting his sister's scarf.
Nearby, a moose snapped the snowman's twig limbs in two. What
kind of barbaric place was this?

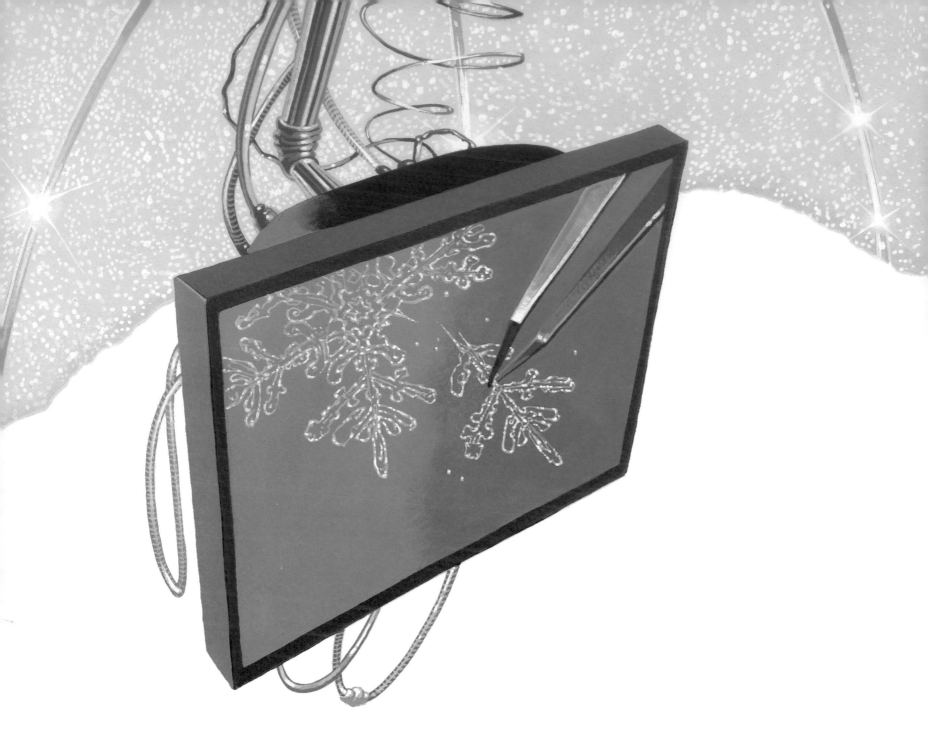

What Owen saw at the next station made him gasp. They had taken apart his snowman, snowflake by snowflake, and now a pointy instrument was tweezing apart each snowflake, branch by branch. Outraged, Owen turned to the polar bear. "How would you like someone to pull off your arms?"

The polar bear hunched a little closer over his microscope. That's when it hit Owen. "Everybody thinks the sun melts snowmen. But they're wrong. Snowmen are just brought here."

"Back off," said the polar bear. "You're too warm."

"What difference does it make if I'm too warm? You're already taking apart the snowman."

"You're getting warmer, Owen," said the chilling voice from the loudspeaker. "Move along now. Exit right. Mind your step."

Owen stepped out onto an open field of snow piled and puffed, wondering if he could still save his snowman. A vehicle hauling a load of carrots was coming up fast. Owen raced to the driver. "Those look perfect," he said, puzzled.

"Yes," said the rabbit. "We grow them here ourselves. They're for snowmen."

"Snowmen?" said Owen. "But I thought you destroy snowmen."

The rabbit stared at Owen. "Why would we destroy snowmen if we grow new noses?"

It began to feel warmer. Up ahead Owen saw a crop of chimneys sticking out of the snow. A white cat leaped onto one and went down. A moment later it reappeared, but now it was black with soot. Held in its small mouth was something round and black.

"What is that you're carrying?" said Owen. The cat's eyes went wide and the thing dropped from its mouth.

Owen caught the lump of coal and turned it over in his hand.

"These are eyes, right? I use buttons, but I know most people use coal."
The cat darted off.

"Eyes, nose, everything like new." Owen called after it, "Hey, are you *making* a snowman?" But the cat was gone. Owen stomped his foot in frustration, and the snow caved in beneath him. He dropped right through . . .

. . . and was pitched into a cloud. Cold gusts blew Owen here and there, setting him to spin and spin. Never had he felt so fine, so fluffed, so wonderful! Owen had dropped into a chamber for making snowflakes.

Suddenly the chamber stopped gusting, and Owen fell onto the cold floor.

Two walruses stared at him.

"Look, he got them all dirty," said one, and sent the snowflakes to be cleaned, every needle, every branch.

"We don't take snowmen apart," said the other, "and clean them top to bottom for nothing, you know."

"So why do you take them apart and clean them?"

The walruses looked at each other and shrugged.

"I know," said Owen. "It's to make the perfect snowman!"

Owen was so pleased with his discovery he thrust his hand back into the chamber and caught a snowflake.

"Don't touch!" said a walrus.

The snowflake melted in Owen's hand.

"See, you're too warm."

"But that's how you build a snowman," said Owen. "With your hands."

At the last station, Owen discovered the pieces of his snowman, all perfectly remade.

A puffin stared up at him. "From top to bottom, we've improved on your snowman," said the puffin. "Only we've had a bit of trouble getting him started." The puffin held the very beginnings of a snowball, and they were very poor beginnings, indeed.

"I'll show you how." Owen scooped up a handful of snow. He held the snow until it got a touch melty from the warmth of his hands. Now the snow rolled nicely into a round ball.

"You roll the best snowball," said the puffin.

"Feel," said Owen, giving the puffin his hand.

The puffin held Owen's hand. "Warm."

One ball at a time, Owen and the puffin made a snowman. As Owen wrapped his sister's scarf around it, the puffin said, "Can I tell you how long we have tried to make a snowman?"

"This is your first?"

The puffin blushed. "Yes."

Owen looked back at the millions of cleaned and improved pieces of other snowmen. "What's all that for?"

"You," said the chilling voice from the loudspeaker. "That's why we brought you here."

Owen looked up. "You brought me here?"

"Yes," said the voice. "You will roll the perfect snowball at the heart of all our snowmen."

Worried, Owen looked around.

Meanwhile, the animals had gathered to see their first snowman.

One pointed at the snowman. "Look, it's melting."

"Not possible!" boomed the voice on the loudspeaker. "At these temperatures a snowman can last forever."

The puffin set up a machine that would uncover the nature of any snowman problem. With a flip of a switch all was revealed. From deep inside the snowman glowed a warm snowball.

"What has the boy done?" said the voice from the loudspeaker. It sounded a little disappointed.

"When a boy makes a snowman, he gives it a heart," said the puffin. "It gets so warm inside, the snowman can't last."

The animals looked at each other. All at once they knew the factory would close, because the only place a snowman would last forever was in a boy's heart.

The next morning was bright and sunny as Owen pulled his sister over
the snow on his new sled. As they passed the snowman, she said, "Look, your
snowman is melting."

"Don't you know, it's not the sun that melts the snowman," said Owen. "It's
his heart."

"Yes," his sister said. "I know."

Owen retrieved her scarf and then pulled them toward the big hill.
His sister noticed the scarf was woven like new. "That's all right," she said,
wrapping it around her. "I'll have it comfy again by next Christmas."